www.hmhco.com

The text of this book is set in Adderville ITC Std.
The illustrations are rendered in scratchboard and watercolor.

Library of Congress Cataloging-in-Publication Data
Sidman, Joyce.
Before morning / by Joyce Sidman ;
illustrated by Beth Krommes.
pages cm
Summary: Let snow fall overnight and change the world before morning,
making it "slow and delightful and white."
ISBN 978-0-547-97917-5 (hardback)
[1. Stories in rhyme. 2. Snow—Fiction. 3. City and town life—Fiction.]
I. Krommes, Beth, illustrator. II. Title.
PZ8.3.S5719Be 2015
[E]—dc23
2014048523
Manufactured in China
SCP 10 9 8 7 6 5 4 3 2 1
4500600153

# Before Morning

by **Joyce Sidman**

illustrated by **Beth Krommes**

HOUGHTON MIFFLIN HARCOURT
Boston  New York

For Gail, my sister and
role model, with memories of
the snow days of our youth.
—J.S.

For my family, who make it
possible for me to pursue
my dreams. —B.K.

In the deep woolen dark,

as we slumber unknowing,

let the sky fill with flurry and flight.

Let the air turn to feathers,

the earth turn to sugar,

Let quick things be swaddled,

let urgent plans founder,

let pathways be hidden from sight.

Please—just this once—

make it slow

and delightful...

and white.

## On Wishes and Invocations

How powerful are words? Can they make things happen? Stop them from happening? Can they protect us? Comfort us? Enchant us? This book is written in the form of an *invocation*—a poem that invites something to happen, often asking for help or support. Humans have been using invocations for thousands of years, to soothe the body and strengthen the soul. Do they work? Maybe. Maybe speaking something out loud is the first step toward making it happen.

What is it you wish for? Find the best words for that wish and speak them aloud. Maybe, in the deep woolen dark, snowflakes will begin to fall . . .  —J.S.